MY READING NEIGHBORHOOD
First-Grade Sight Word Stories

Ana and the Pet Show

Sara E. Hoffmann

illustrated by Katie Strange

Consultant:

Marla Conn, MS, Education
Reading/Literacy Specialist

LernerClassroom™
MINNEAPOLIS

I am Ana. I live on First Street.

We are having a pet show here.
It will be so much fun!

Sam will bring his dog, Snow.

I will bring my cat, Lulu.

Joe will bring Nosy.

He belongs to Ms. Green from next door.

Snow barks. Lulu gets scared.
Nosy sleeps and sleeps.

They are all winners anyway!